MW01248465

Mark Andrews

MY BITCH OF A MISTRESS

FETISH WORLD BOOKS

Chapter 1

I was lucky to be born with good genes that gave me a fine physique and a reasonably good brain, allowing me to breeze through high school, excelling at all sports but particularly gymnastics and obtaining good grades scholastically as well.

One of my school fellows was Frederica Masters and although physically she was an incredible looker and like me, excelled at all sports with a faintly muscular body, and excelled at her studies as well, she was really a real bitch at heart.

Unlike me, who was born of middle-class parents who both worked at the local milk company, my father being a driver and my mother working in the factory, Frederica was born to money – real money. I believe her parents were billionaires and they lived on a very small island in the Broadwater of Southport, their beautiful house being the only property on the island.

Her parents were actually very nice people although I think they doted on their daughter, their only child, to the point she was spoiled rotten and believed she had the right to lord it over everyone around her.

Because we were both bright academically and excelled at sports she decided that I was going to be her boyfriend. Unfortunately for me, I cordially despised her and shunned her rather imperious statement that she had chosen me over all the others in our group. She didn't show it outwardly at that time, but inwardly I discovered later she flew into a rage and swore to 'get me' when the opportunity presented itself.

And for the remainder of our school life, she either ignored me or smirked at me as I passed and cast aspersions on my character and my background to her sycophantic friends all of whom smirked and/or giggled in support of her insulting comments. I simply ignored them.

Apart from her, my school life was pleasing and during it I formed a desire to become a journalist and by dint of holiday jobs at *The Bulletin*, achieved a cadetship with that local paper upon graduating from high school. The cadetship included studying journalism at Griffith University and I thought my life was on a fine trajectory...

Alas, I hadn't reckoned with Frederica's malice and intention to bring me down – hard! She planned it well. She couldn't have known that her parents were both going to die tragically from eating infected oysters and although she and their butler and his wife (being the only paid servants on the island) immediately called an ambulance and a doctor, nothing could save them and they both died within a day or so of the symptoms emerging.

She was their only child and inherited the whole estate amounting to some twenty billion dollars which of course included the island and its beautiful house. I now believe that getting back at me was the most important consideration in her life and while she appeared to be perfectly normal in her relations with other people, deep down, she wanted revenge for what she considered was a major slight to her self-importance.

It was only a month or two after her parents' funeral that she sprang the trap. She sent invitations to a summer barbecue at her home, stipulating that

6

swimming gear was the only clothing necessary. I thought it a little strange and in any case would not have accepted the invitation except that after a few years, it might be good to catch up with old school friends whom I hadn't seen since those school years.

Accordingly, and dressing only in the brief nylon swimming togs I preferred, I made my way to the island and was received with apparent friendship by her. The party centred around the swimming pool and we were very well waited upon by an army of slaves under the direction of Mr and Mrs Havers.

Of course, in the nature of those parties, eventually we all stripped off what little clothing remained and cavorted rather salaciously with the others, Mr and Mrs Havers now having departed to their own quarters

During the party, Frederica invited individuals into the house for various reasons and eventually it was my turn. I didn't particularly want to go anywhere with her but politeness demanded that I do so. It was a fateful decision and led to my total and complete downfall. She had planned it down to the last detail. She had secreted a quantity of her vaginal juices in a handy spot on her dressing table and when we entered the room she led me over there, smeared those juices all over my cock and then screamed "Rape!" at the top of her voice, whereupon her friends, already primed, rushed in and secured me while another rang the police.

I'm sure you can imagine what followed. I had no chances at all. Frederica was well known as the heir to the Masters fortune. I was caught with her vaginal juices on my weapon and I was arrested on the spot and taken away just as I was, still stark naked and already looking like a criminal slave who, as you well know, are not permitted any clothing whatsoever.

I well remember the fateful words of the police inspector who led the small group of police who arrived: "Peter Franklin, you are under arrest for the crime of rape…"

I'm sorry to say that my parents were of little help during that dreadful time leading to the trial. They didn't come to see me and provided me with no clothes and the police were quite happy to leave me naked in the holding cell surrounded by other men who constantly attempted to fuck me. The cops even stood and watched outside the iron bars, grinning as those other men attempted to get me down and their cocks in my arse. They all thought I was a rapist and as such had no compassion whatsoever for me.

They did provide me with clothing for my trial which of course was an open and shut case resulting in me being found guilty and sentenced to slavery for the rest of my life as a result.

No-one believed my story, not even my parents. I was now alone and having been sentenced, was stripped naked by the bailiff there in front of everyone in the court including my parents. They watched, stone-faced as he tore each item from my body and then left the court. I never saw them again.

Having been sentenced and stripped, I was now returned to the holding cell wherein were the other prisoners, each as naked as me as, unless you were sentenced to a fine, criminal slavery was the only other alternative and that involved permanent nakedness.

Nakedness means no clothing but that wasn't all of it: slaves were also denuded of all facial and body hair to add to the shame and humiliation associated with criminal slavery, however that state was achieved at the State Slave Centre (SSC) and in the meantime we awaited the even more shameful walk from the courthouse to that building, situated over two kilometres from it.

I knew what it involved – everybody did. And so when the court finally closed at three o'clock, the guard came for us, bring us out of the cell one by one and locking a special genital cuff around the root of our cocks and balls and chaining them together with the chain coming forward from the newly made slave behind and between our legs.

We were then led out of the courthouse where waited the usual gathering of ghouls who delighted in the shame and humiliation of all newly made slaves.

I should comment here that there were a couple of females amongst the half-dozen or so rest of us and their chaining was achieved by the piercing of the left side of their vaginal lips and the insertion of a lockable ring through the newly made hole.

And yes, if you think that Frederica was among that group of despicable people, you would be dead right. She situated herself right near me, licking her lips and smiling in triumph as she beheld my total shame and humiliation. And what is more, she followed us all the way to the SSC and seemed quite disappointed that they were not permitted entry to watch for the next stage of our descent from free citizenship of Australia to an abject criminal slave.

Of course she had enormous pull and I wasn't at all surprised to see her, alone of all the crowd who had followed us from the courthouse, coming in behind us, eager to see me stripped of my natural hair and thus physically converted to a state of slavery.

She wasn't interested in the others whom I noticed merely passed through a machine that zapped them (they were given a sort of rubber bathing To protect the hair on their heads). I'm told it is a relatively painless operation and is permanent. But rapists are another question and I was held until last and then ordered up onto a table and my limbs stretched out to its corners and chained in place and then two slaves were issued with tweezers and ordered to pluck me clean of all hair from my moustache down. This was possible because I had not been permitted to shave from the time of my arrest and my moustache and beard had grown sufficiently to allow plucking.

It was horrible. Most of us have plucked a hair or two from our bodies from time to time and it is relatively painless, isn't it? But you try plucking all of the hairs at one time and that is a very different question. The thing is, I now understood that rapists even more than murderers are held in such high contempt that nothing is too horrible when it came to punishing them. It was pointless me protesting that I had been framed for they simply wouldn't have believed me. Frederica is not only an extremely beautiful and wealthy young woman but also oozes sincerity and innocence and there is not a single person in the world who would have believed me over her.

She stood there beside the table on which I was secured and gloated as she beheld the pain becoming worse and worse every second as those two slaves worked to pluck every visible hair on my body and they were also encouraged to feel and fondle my muscles and my cock and balls as much as they liked – and this pair obviously did like!

In fact, the officers present even encouraged them to actually suck my cock from time to time and then called me a queer as it responded to their ministrations and erected to its full 22 centimetre length.

And still Frederica stood there gloating but otherwise silent as she watched my body being slowly but carefully stripped of all its natural hair. But that wasn't the worst of it. I am not an overly hairy person (or rather I wasn't) but I had underarm hair, a small smattering on my chest, my pubic growth, and of course that on my lower legs and these areas were now extremely sensitive from the ministrations of those two slaves working on my body while tormenting me or playing with and sucking my cock.

What came next was even worse. Simply plucking the hairs would not prevent them from re-growing and so what they now did was to smear a horribly smelling greasy substance over those areas they had now plucked and immediately they did so, the skin started to burn as if they had spread hydrochloric acid on them. It burned and burned and burned and I flailed around as much as the chains holding my wrists and ankles permitted and

11

screamed while Frederica moved even closer almost drooling as she watched my pain and humiliation.

The trial was held on a Tuesday and I thus had Tuesday night to Saturday morning in the SSC before my body would be put up for auction. This time was spent in a ruthless round of exercising just about every single part of the body all day, every day. There was nothing else.

For security purposes, a tiny sliver of silicon was inserted onto the right testicle of every male and the inner moist flesh of the clitoris of a female. This was achieved very simply with us males by simply making a tiny slit in the scrotal wall, peeling the wax paper off the glued side of the chip and placing it onto the actual testicle itself, and then applying a Band-Aid to the small wound in the scrotum. This chip functioned as a GPS locator but could also receive signals from the slave's owner which included a punishment zap that would have him or her down on the ground in a foetal ball screaming for release from the pain.

We slept in a huge room whose concrete floor was painted into virtual cells one metre wide by two metres long and once placed in there and the system activated, even a limb moving over the painted boundary of your cell automatically activated this punishment zap and so one learned very quickly never to let any part of one's body stray from that cell.

Of course we were fed the universal slave food, Slave Chow which was both cheap and simple to provide. It is made from inexpensive foods of every class in exactly the right proportions and including minerals and vitamins, all stewed together in huge pressure cookers and then masticated into a smooth paste and exuded in half centimetre diameter tubes, dried and cut off at one centimetre lengths. It is very cheap to produce and a double handful night and morning followed by as much water as the slave can take in, is a perfect diet, although rather unpleasant for the recipient.

But then, from six in the morning until nine at night every single one of us then resident in the SSC was put through an extremely demanding round of exercises of every shape and size imaginable, the only relief in that fifteen hour session being to drop in genuine exhaustion whereupon the whip was applied to restore the guilty slave to the workout.

It is totally inhuman – by design. This whole regime underlines to the newly made slave that he is no longer considered as a human being. Like every other child, it had been dinned into me at home and school that the situation across the world by the middle of the 21st-century was so bad that only the admittedly draconian regime that was criminal slavery would be sufficient to curb the crime wave and religious terror that had come very close to destroying humanity. And it did this very much by the horrible nature and conditions that criminal slavery imposed.

If one is contemplating purchasing a slave, he must be sure that he has the ability and opportunity to impose a regime of hard labour for the minimum fifteen hours per day, seven days a week, no exceptions, that is required of a criminal slave. This is to be continued unchecked for at least a year but may then be continued further at the owner's discretion if he believes it is necessary or even if he simply wishes it to continue for his own gratification.

I well knew that Frederica had engineered this whole scenario in order to obtain control over me and my body and that once she did, I would be facing a life of pain, humiliation and horror. Nothing would be beyond her revenge and as I thought about it, I wondered at her sanity.

Yes, she had been indulged to the point of stupidity by doting parents but I don't believe that either explained or justified her unreasoned hatred of me simply because I didn't wish to be her boyfriend. Of course there was nothing I could do about it. I was now a slave which meant that I had now lost not only my citizenship of Australia, but also my very humanity. Nothing was too bad for a slave! Not that I was or even am critical of this situation. The world had come so close to a total breakdown of civilisation and criminal slavery had rectified that situation almost instantly. No sane person today would even dream of even easing the lot of a slave under this regime.

I was caught in a system that allowed no relief, even from a totally sadistic owner. I don't think Frederica harboured such thoughts about other people but so far as I was concerned, nothing would be beyond the pale when it came to satisfying her so-called humiliation that I had rejected her.

I was lucky in one sense that my body was as well honed from a life of sports and hard exercise that I had continued as best I could during my cadetship with the newspaper. It meant that I could actually relish the hard exercise and know that it was honing and toning my muscles even in those few days at the SSC and so when I came to be placed on the block in the auction room on that fateful Saturday morning I stared up at the countless hundreds of registered bidders seated in the semicircular, tiered rows of chairs facing the auction block that traditionally is simply a butt of a large tree trunk, a half metre high and on which the slave has to stand and pose his or her body in accordance with a sequence in which they are trained so as to show it off to best example.

Bidding on a slave starts at one hundred thousand dollars and may be advanced by any sum a bidder desires but this is achieved by means of a small unit issued and registered to him or her as they enter the auction room and is connected to the computer controlling the sale and also to his or her bank account so that payment may be made at the moment of sale.

I stood there with a knot in my stomach searching around the audience for Frederica but wasn't surprised to see her in the centre of the first row. She was staring up at me in triumph. She had the resources to pay any sum at all for my body and I knew she wouldn't care if it was even a million dollars.

But she was no fool. I may have had a good body but so did many other slaves and the bidding moved up in lots of between two and ten thousand dollars until she tired of it and added another hundred thousand to the last sum. This so stunned the other bidders that I was awarded to her by default, she effected payment immediately, and I became her property.

The knot in my stomach now solidified to a

huge stone and I shuddered as I thought of what the future now held for me over on that beautiful island that was going to become my prison and torture chamber.

My trials and tribulations started immediately.

She had brought a slave with her and as she moved up to the clerk to take possession of my body she gestured to this young male slave (no person can be enslaved until they are at least eighteen years old but anyone from 19 to 29 may be considered young in slave parlance) to hand her up my first restraint.

This was a heavy steel hinged collar that had bars with wrist manacles extending out either side of it. She opened this and fitted it around my neck then closed and locked it and then secured each wrist in the steel manacle so that my arms were held up and out from my shoulders.

She then bent over and secured one of the special steel manacles designed for the root of the scrotum and penis of a male slave, that has a chain attached to it and then simply led me out of the SSC and into its car park where waited a new vehicle she had had designed and built just for me.

I stared at this and the knot in my stomach started punching itself. It wasn't very complicated being simply an axle with twenty-eight inch bicycle wheels to which an aluminium alloy pole about a metre long had been bolted and braced. A quite comfortable seat had been bolted to the axle. Nothing very remarkable about this, you think? And so far at least, I would agree with you. But it was what she had had built onto the end of it that had me staring in horror.

About two centimetres back from the very end an extremely realistic hard rubber, flesh coloured male human penis poked up and forward – and it was all of twenty centimetres long! And right in front of that at the very end of the pole was yet another of those manacles designed for the genitals of a male human being.

There could be no doubt what I was now facing but just to underline it to me, she stopped right in front of this horrible arrangement on the end of the pole and turned and smiled sweetly at me.

"Just think, boy, how wonderful it's going to be for you to feel that huge fake cock up your arse as you gallop me home to the island, and just so you know that I may encourage you when you falter or slow down, that cock is electrified as is the manacle around your cock and balls, and I understand that the shock will have you screaming in agony.

"Don't worry however, I know that incredible body has both the capacity and the endurance to gallop me all the way home and then it will be time to give you your welcome to my new ownership of you.

"Wonderful is it not, boy?"

Aware that if I didn't answer she would shock me anyway, I replied in the affirmative. "Yes, Mistress. Wonderful indeed."

She looked at me closely, trying to find even a hint of guile in my words or expression. There was none. I knew I was beaten and that resistance wouldn't help my future one little bit. She now owned me legally for the rest of my life and because the sentence was indeed for the whole of my life, she could have me modified in any way she saw fit short of killing me. She could have me castrated, either just my balls or if she wished, my cock, too. She could have my arms removed or perhaps my legs. She could torture me in any way she saw fit even without reason.

In short she had me exactly where she wanted me and I now reasoned that my best course of action was compliance with her will.

She positioned me over the end of the pole, having first had me lubricate it with my spit – and made me dive right down on it, and then I had to stand up, turn around and submit to having it forced up into my rectum. Naturally, she wasn't going to bother herself with my sensibilities and simply pushed it up hard, gloating as I screamed at the pain of this first anal intrusion by a foreign body into my arsehole.

And then, when it was all the way in, she closed the cuff around my cock and balls, tightening it click by click until it was just a shade overly-tight and then locked it. This had the effect of causing an erection which she grabbed and toyed with for a few seconds then remarked that she had not given me permission to erect and I would therefore be further punished upon us arriving at her home.

I didn't comment at the unfairness of this because by now I knew that every moment of my life from that moment on was going to be one or another variety of hell and the best way I could cope with it was to simply try to absorb the shame and pain but make every attempt to let her see just how distressed her actions were making me.

I reasoned that she would eventually tire of my screams and moans and writhings and every other way of showing her how she was getting to me.

Having firmly secured me to her new gig and mounted up, she now ordered me to take off and head for the bridge leading to her island. "And I want it to be a gallop, at least when road conditions permit it, slave! Slacking will not be permitted at any time."

I gulped. Yes, I was as fit as the proverbial Mallee bull but pulling her merely by that plug up my arse and the cuff around my cock and balls would surely destroy those organs permanently?

But slaves have no discretion. An order is an order. Very much the same as the Roman army ordered to march off the edge of a cliff into the sea upon the orders of Caesar, simply on his whim.

I took off and was surprised that even with my arms outstretched by that horrible thing around my neck, I was able to get up quite a pace and I even found that the method of anchoring that little gig to my body didn't really pose much strain on it at all. Although I had never in my life even contemplated having any form of sexual relations with another man, I have to admit that I actually found the pressure of that fake cock up my arse and the ring around my cock and balls to be rather exciting – sexually, that is.

I'm not saying that I was actively contemplating having sex with a male. That idea was still a most unpleasant one but the physical feelings within my anus and the pressure around the root of my cock and balls were quite bearable and actually rather pleasant.

As these thoughts roved through my mind on that journey towards the island along the Esplanade,

I began to see that what I must now do was to try to enjoy every humiliation and painful activity she ordered for me but ensure that on the surface I was showing the appropriate level of pain and humiliation to satisfy her insane demands for retribution for my so-called rudeness to her.

You are shocked? Don't be. I was merely trying to work out how best to cope with what I expected to be the most horrible existence any human being could impose on another. I wondered then what Mr and Mrs Havers would make of her singling me out for extreme painful and humiliating punishments with no apparent reason.

What I hadn't understood is that as lifelong servants to her family, they mightn't approve but they certainly wouldn't object. Remember that the law was quite explicit in that criminal slaves had no rights whatsoever and if an owner went beyond the pale in his or her treatment of a slave, then that was just too bad for that slave.

In thinking about this, I imagined that as time passed, the severity of the punishments open to slave owners may be adjusted somewhat but at that moment, that certainly wasn't the case and for me, anything and everything she could drum up to humiliate me was perfectly acceptable.

As I galloped her along, I felt the presence of that huge plug up my arse beginning to give me pleasure and at that moment, I actually understood why a gay bottom so much appreciates being fucked in this manner. Not that I was looking for it. At that moment, while I was still exclusively heterosexual, I also recognised that Frederica would be very likely to order me to make homosexual love to another man or vice versa as an after-dinner entertainment.

This is something that developed quite early in the era of criminal slavery. Slaves have always been relatively expensive and only the moneyed class of person could afford them. However when the idea of using slaves to put on entertainments after a dinner party first manifested itself, it wasn't long before they became sexual in nature and after that, homosexual events between strictly heterosexual participants became very amusing to the watching guests.

I reasoned that as she well knew how much I hated the idea of homosexual activity as evidenced by this method of harnessing that parodied it so well, it wouldn't be very long before I was going to have to perform in such an event with one of the male slaves in her household.

Of course, being among the wealthiest of families in Australia, her parents had been able to afford the very best slaves to serve them. Money was no object and therefore their slaves were all either beautiful or highly attractive females and either muscular or athletic as well as good-looking males all of whom I knew had very large genital equipment while the females generally had vulvae of the flat and vertical slit kind, these being considered the most attractive for a naked female slave.

I didn't think Frederica would be very likely to order me to fuck one of the female slaves. Really I didn't think she would want to see me fucking anything…

What would give her most pleasure was to

watch me fucked either by one of her male slaves with the largest cock and balls or perhaps, by one of her outdoor female slaves, a couple of whom were decidedly muscular, equipped with one of those strap on dildo arrangements that have a smallish element that goes inside their vaginas but with a huge, sometimes ribbed external member designed to give horrible pain to the recipient.

All these thoughts were ranging through my mind as I conveyed her along the Esplanade towards the bridge to her island. Because of the traffic I could sometimes spurt ahead at my best speed but at other times had to slow down and this gave me a chance for my lungs to recover somewhat but of course I wondered what she was thinking as she sat in that comfortable chair watching my naked body and of course particularly my buttocks as they were split apart by that huge dong up my arse.

I didn't have any idea but I did note that she didn't zap me in order to encourage a faster pace at any time and so I assumed she was at least satisfied if not happy with my performance as her new pony slave.

Such a use of slaves by the wealthy had become relatively common but to my knowledge no-one had dreamed up her bizarre method of harnessing their slave to the gig. That I was coping with it was I think a measure of my own physical fitness. Over and over again, I marvelled that the initial pain of the intrusion into my arsehole had now completely abated and that I was deriving some pleasure from the constant moving around of that fake penis up there.

I was aware though that this was a very new

thing for my body and I wondered how long it might be before I began to feel pain from the abrasion of that huge thing inserted right up my backside. At least so far, there was no pain at all, now.

And that thought led me to wonder how to cope if and when she had me on the receiving end of a male to male fucking as one of her after-dinner entertainments. As I said before, I knew I would have to pretend to outrage and pain and humiliation and wondered how good an actor I might be if the act with a real man was as pleasurable as what I was feeling at that moment.

My thoughts then ranged to the male slaves on the island and I gulped as I recalled one of them in particular: his name was Roger and he was very tall – around two metres I guessed – and very muscular in an athletic rather than a bodybuilding way. His muscles were extremely well defined and rippled rather dramatically every time he moved. He was black and his skin a beautiful dark chocolate colour. He was also a very nice man as I knew from the times I had been to a party there and he had been serving us.

Although he is possibly the very best example of a male human I had ever seen, I still wasn't attracted to him sexually. However, if it transpired that she chose him to fuck me or vice versa, I knew I could do it and perhaps even derive some pleasure from it but that must be an absolute no-no! I would have to scream and protest and fight and do my best to show my abhorrence of such an act with a man. As she watched this performance of mine I knew she would delight in my shame and humiliation and as my mind continue to work on this theme, I knew therein lay my best choice for my immediate future on her island.

Chapter 2

Once home, she lost no time in scheduling my Welcome. If you're not familiar with this term in the sense of a slave, it means a particularly nasty punishment such as a caning or perhaps electro-genital punishment to the testicles and/or penis and is meant to make the slave aware of what he might expect if he errs under this new ownership of his body.

In her case, she favours the cane. It is an instrument of punishment that has been used for centuries to punish and correct errant schoolchildren, servants and sometimes even wives and has been resurrected for use on slaves and in this case is even more thoroughly applied both in severity and the number of strokes to be delivered although generally the buttocks are the preferred destination.

In modern times, rather than having the slave bend over and touch his or her toes, an item described as a punishment bench or caning bench has been developed and may be found in any household containing slaves.

In most cases it is based on those old wooden forms once used in school classrooms before the advent of individual desks for students and is usually twenty-five centimetres wide, three metres long and its top surface is usually about fifty centimetres above the floor height.

At the bottom corners Velcro manacles for the ankles are fitted so that the feet dangle over the edge while at the very top extremities very sturdy hooks have been screwed securely into the timber angled so that a chain connected to wrist manacles may be slipped over them to securely hold the slave in position for the punishment.

This was what I faced as she led me into the slave quarters in the cellars of that beautiful house.

Mr and Mrs Havers had assembled the rest of the slaves to witness my Welcome and they were lined up on one side of the punishment bench on which she now directed me to lay my body face down. Mrs Havers saw to my ankles while her husband attended to my wrists so that I was stretched out as tightly as he could get me after which he moved over to a huge brass shell casing containing a dozen or more rattan canes and selected one and handed it to his employer.

Rattan is a cane that grows in the jungles of Malaya and has been used for centuries as the perfect instrument of correction for the human body. It is flexible but very sturdy and unlike bamboo, which tends to shatter after a dozen or so strokes, may be used over and over again. As an instrument for administering pain to the human buttocks it is beyond compare and I have to admit that I was now extremely fearful of the coming hurt, especially as I knew that Frederica, with her extremely athletic body and its muscles, would be applying every last milligram of power to each of the strokes she was about to administer to my body.

She hadn't mentioned how many that would be in number and I guessed that had been intentional and that she would continue to cane me until she thought I had had enough.

I did notice that unlike in the past where they had seemed very contented in her service during the parties I had attended there in very much more happy circumstances than was the case now, they all looked most apprehensive and I wondered if she had become more sadistic in her punishment for their offences than had been the case before.

But such wonderings didn't last long. In my position lying along that bench, she was behind me and all I heard was a light gasp from one or more of the slaves that was followed by the slight whistle of the tip of the cane through the air and then I felt the blow, fair across the crown of both cheeks of my buttocks.

In line with the rest of my rather athletic body, those two joint muscles are of the type often described as bubble-butt, are quite narrow and hollowed out on their outer sides and were a perfect target for her sadistic lust. I had been expecting it but I wasn't prepared for the degree of pain that now manifested itself centring on my buttocks but seeming to spread outwards from that point to every other part of my body. The pain was horrible – absolutely terrible but I slammed my lips closed and ground my teeth together and tensioned every muscle in my body in an effort to contain the pain inside me and not to give her the pleasure of hearing me scream and perhaps even begging for it to stop.

I know I had resolved to go along with everything she wanted from me but for some reason I knew it was the right thing to show some courage at this time. In any case the straining of the muscles all over my body was enough of an aphrodisiac to give her pleasure from my body and I sensed her stepping back to watch how I coped with the first of God knows how many such strokes there would be.

"He shows some spirit, Havers," she said brightly. "Well I will just have to try harder, won't I?"

"Indeed, Madam," he said. "Perhaps he will take some taming, do you think?"

"I certainly hope so. He was my guest at that party and then raped me and I am going to ensure he is well punished for his crime…"

I lay there and listened to this lie and I think it was then that I knew that nothing I did was going to alleviate the pain and humiliation she was going to heap on me day after day after day.

Stroke number two followed that little dialogue and Havers congratulated her on how thoroughly she was correcting me for my horrible crime against her. Again I managed to bite back any vocal reaction to the pain but again my body struggled and strained against the manacles and chains holding me down to that bench.

Welcomes were usually token punishments simply to make the slave aware of what he or she faced if they erred but in Frederica's case she wanted me to suffer the horrors of the damned and I certainly did.

She is very strong and she applied every last milligram of her considerable strength into making every one of those strokes give me exquisite pain, which was now mounting cumulatively, one after the other. She ceased after twelve during which I had managed to contain my pain without uttering a sound – which didn't please her one little bit – or so I thought.

Why did I do this when I had earlier formed a policy of appeasing her? To be honest, I don't know. Something in me just told me to be strong about this and to bear it without uttering a murmur. Later I discovered that it was indeed the right thing to do. It created in her a small level of respect for my fortitude and that it was this and no other reason that she ceased after delivering twelve strokes so perhaps my intuition was serving me well.

She even ordered Mrs Havers to treat my buttocks with her special ointment which I was to discover had an almost magical ability to heal and to ease the pain. I was then left there to sleep off that horrible welcome.

But that didn't mean my trials and tribulations were over. Not by a long shot. The next day, with my buttocks largely healed, she came for me early in the morning and led me out to the garden where she sought out her head garden slave and asked him where the next compost pit was to be dug.

He didn't even turn a hair, knowing his mistress as well as he did, he knew she was planning another penance for me and led her over to his nursery area behind the house and pointed to a spot within the hedged confines. "This area contains a mixture of clay and sand, Mistress. It works very well to create good new soil when we place new garden waste and lawn clippings in there. Do you need someone to supervise him, ma'am?"

"No. I can program his chip to keep him working all day or until I switch it off. If he even takes a rest for a second or two, he will be zapped…"

She gestured to me to begin digging in the area the slave now marked out and showed me where to deposit the soil from the diggings. I gulped. I have never been shy of work or exercise but what she was demanding of me now promised to be as bad an exercise as I could have ever contemplated.

Everyone has often joked about labourers resting on their shovels more than actually working. I think the issue of whether a human body can indeed work non-stop at physical labour for hour after hour is moot but I didn't want to be the test subject in such an experiment. Nevertheless, I knew this was just one of the horrible tortures she had already dreamed up for me and no doubt was already thinking up new ones to make my life as totally unbearable as she could.

By now I was very definitely of the opinion that she was mad. All this simply because I had refused her attentions and invitation to be her boyfriend all those years ago? Does this sound like the actions of a sane person? I certainly didn't think so but of course I was the only one who knew the whole story. Everyone else simply thought I had violated her at that party on this island and I was now receiving my just rewards.

I couldn't blame them. In their case, I would think the same.

In any case, she now activated my chip and so my labour had to begin or I would suffer that horrible zap to my testicle. I started in my bare feet, by now sufficiently hardened to use on the spade and began digging out the mixture of soil and clay and heaping it as directed.

Hour after hour I continued. Where did I get the strength to keep going without a single break? I have no idea. I just dug and heaved and dug and heaved and dug and heaved, on and on, hour after hour, slowly lowering the hole but ensuring that the sides remained square and so far as possible with that sandy mixture, kept then straight and smooth.

From time to time, she came down and stood on the side of the developing pit, watching me critically but at no time did I stop the action of digging and heaving although every muscle in my body was now aching horribly and it came the time, sometime in the afternoon I judged from the position of the sun above my head, when I just collapsed, my body and its muscles and cardiovascular system now totally exhausted.

No doubt my chip was zapping my testicle but I was too far gone to feel it, or perhaps she had switched it off. She directed the garden slave to hose me down and of course that woke me up at which I grabbed for the spade but only managed to dig one spadeful and then my muscles simply seized up and whilst I didn't lose consciousness this time, I just stood there and stared up at her standing on the edge of the pit, sneering down at my weakness.

At that moment, good sense and reason had left me and I believed she was right. Now thinking about it in hindsight, I would suggest that that particular exercise might even stand as a record for any one person toiling non-stop at hard physical labour. I suspect it must have been at least eight! Not that I am boasting. It was labour performed under perhaps the worst that could be applied to a male human – horribly painful electric shocks to his testicle!

I have heard of electrical torture to these organs being used by intelligence agencies – and not only those of our enemies, either. I'm not making accusations. What I've heard is just rumour. Nevertheless I can testify from my own experience that the threat of that pain was what kept me going hour after hour in horrible fear that I would fail and be made to bear it.

On that occasion I couldn't even climb out of the pit and she had to send her gardener down to help me out, directing him to take me to the quarters and allow me to sleep it off. I think I slept for twelve hours before she appeared to apprise me of my next penance.

This was punishment for my crime of erecting my cock when she teased it.

As you might imagine, to make the punishment fit the crime, so to speak, she had me spreadeagled in the slave punishment gallows out at the back of the house. She then fitted a rubber bag filled with ice blocks over my genitals so that they were fully and totally enclosed in the solid blocks of ultra cold ice and then tied it off.

"These may take an hour to thaw," she directed the kitchen slave. "But then I want them replaced with fresh ice blocks – and that is to continue all day."

I gulped. Have you ever had ice blocks pressed to a part of your body? It's really strange but you think you are being burned. And apparently I had now to contend with that awful pain all day. And remember I was also subject to the distress of being suspended in a spreadeagle so that my body was displayed in a perfect 'X', which is painful enough in itself.

The bag that was tied around my genitals was

in the form of one of those little bags in which a lady keeps her cosmetics when she goes travelling and has a drawstring at the top. This one was sturdier than those being made of thick rubber that tended to insulate the ice blocks from the effects of the external temperature but it was very copious holding a great number of the blocks below the lowest extremity of my balls and this meant that the freezing ice blocks continued to apply this horrible – really horrible torture all day.

She came down regularly to stand and stare at me, gloating at my body spreadeagled in that so painful position but moving up often and stroking it with the tips of her fingers apparently deriving sexual pleasure from my muscles and the way they were reacting to my suspension and of course the awful pain being created by those freezing ice blocks.

"This gives me an idea for another punishment for you, boy," she said gloatingly. "I think I will have a refrigeration unit built so that the refrigerating copper pipes may be coiled around your whole body so that when the unit is switched on, they will freeze and gradually refrigerate your body.

"We will have a special part designed for your cock and balls so that they are frozen solid first. Once that occurs, I may tap them with my finger and they will simply drop off, leaving you a total castrate – no cock and no balls! Wouldn't that be a wonderful idea, boy?"

Leaving me with that possibility, she turned on her heels and walked back into the house. By now it was middle afternoon and once again I was very close to the end of my tether. How long can I last these terrible tortures, I wondered. They must be having an effect not only on my body but even more importantly on my mind.

I pulled myself together and angrily castigated myself – at least mentally. 'This is no way to cope with all that she is doing to you', I said to myself. 'You must learn to meet every trial as if it is a physical exercise of your body…'

By that, I meant that just as an athlete pushes his muscles, his cardiovascular system and his mind to deliver just that little bit more in the athletic pursuit he is engaged in, so must I now force my mind and my body to treat these admittedly terrible tortures simply as exercises. And in so doing I would beat her, one way or the other.

Through all of this I kept very alert, not only to the many slaves performing various duties in and out of the house but also on William and Mary Havers and after a few more days I began to see expressions of doubt as the punishments became more and more horrible.

And so far as the slaves were concerned, as the days progressed that formerly happy expression on their faces was replaced with worry that they too might well be exposed to the kind of punishments being meted out to me on a daily basis.

I also kept a watch on Frederica herself. I was now definitely of the opinion that she had suffered some mental trauma that had totally unhinged her mind when it came to me. She continued to treat the Havers' with the same friendliness and courtesy she always had and the other slaves in the appropriate way an owner is supposed to interact with them.

It was only with me that she showed this insane desire to punish in the worst and most horrible ways she could dream up as if I was the devil personified. Why this might be I had no idea but neither was I in any position to do anything about it. At least not yet.

I began to see that as her malady developed even further, she might well invite some of our former school friends to come and observe the way she was punishing me for my perfidy in refusing her offer to be my girlfriend all those years ago. I was sure that if this happened, they would immediately see that she was mad and might even question the notion that I had abused her.

My previous behaviour as a school friend of them all, would surely make them remember how much I had always helped less gifted or well off students than myself and had never, not ever made improper advances to any female at all.

Yes, all this depended on her coming to that stage and I thought that the Havers' were a more likely possibility, but then I also knew that if I once mentioned it and they jumped the wrong way, I might be sealing my own fate for good.

Accordingly, I did nothing but steel my mind and my body to her no longer daily tortures as she now realised that I was in no condition to be subjected to them with such regularity. Instead, on the days she didn't actually schedule me for torture or 'punishment', as she called it, I was put to rigorous exercising both in her private gymnasium and in racing her around and around the island or over to the mainland in her dinky little gig with that horrible plug up my arse and the constraining cuff around my genitals.

I say horrible after earlier reporting that I found its present in my backside quite pleasant that first time. I now realised that had been an aberration, perhaps generated by my psyche to protect me from it. Now however on the occasions she used my anus to punish me, I felt nothing but pain and a sickness that I was being so used.

By now, a few weeks had passed and my punishment days were even more widely spread than the others wherein she ensured that my body was exercised to the absolute maximum possible so as to keep it in the best possible condition.

And these 'free' days allowed my mind to cope with the 'punishments' so-called that she inflicted on the other days. So far, she had not entertained guests to dinner and so there had been no need for an entertainment to follow the meal. I was dreading having to perform sexually, probably with another male, in such an entertainment but I well knew that if she did have guests, I would definitely be scheduled to perform in some disgusting or horrible way.

And of course that is exactly what happened…

She did stage a dinner party, but the guests were not from her usual circle of friends, instead inviting my friends of both genders, indicating that she thought they might be interested in how I was now suffering for her so-called 'rape' by me.

Actually, it was a Sunday barbecue but this time being now in the cooler months, clothing stipulated was simply casual.

You may be wondering how I and the other slaves coped with cold weather and rain periods? The fact is, that as slaves we were not given any protection from them whatsoever and were required to continue working in the rain and cold, stark naked and without any protection to our bodies at all. This was seen as a most salutary part of the punishment of criminal slavery but in fact, I found that my body soon acclimatised itself to the cooling weather patterns and even when she made me toil at some task out in the rain, I found that I soon got used to it, as of course did all of her other outdoor slaves.

But to get back to that barbecue, my first humiliation was to be made to perform a most demeaning dance for them as they sat around the barbecue eating their steaks and salads.

To make it even more shameful, she forced me to wear a tail made from silicon so that it waved around very realistically when shaken by its anal plug. This was in the form of a large ribbed butt-plug whose outer fitting had a 60° angle to it so that the tail inserted into its receptacle poked up and out from the top of the crevice between the buttocks cheeks unlike a real tail if we actually possessed them. The tail itself had been made to parody what a human tail might look like and you could buy them in a colour to match various skin complexions. The one she chose for me matched my skin colour perfectly and so it looked to be a legitimate part of my body even if an extremely bizarre one.

I now had to wear this at all times except when actually defecating but a good part of my day was now spent in learning to dance an extremely suggestive number that parodied the act of human intercourse and of course made my tail flail around wildly as I performed the fuck-fuck dance as she called it.

She always led me in those lessons and practice sessions until she was satisfied that I could perform it for an hour or two while her guests, my former friends sat and watched my shame.

The event was every bit as humiliating as I had expected. There wasn't a single one of them who refused her invitation and I wondered just how good a friend each of them really was to me.

As I made my entry to the barbecue area she ordered me to move around to each of them in turn and to assume The Position. This is the first of a number of positions of slavery and involves the slave parting his feet exactly half a metre, then raising his hands and clasping them behind the back of his head, ensuring that his elbows are pulled as far back as he can get them and then fixing his gaze on some distant object while flexing all the muscles capable of being controlled in this position.

It is a perfect posture to allow for an in-depth inspection of a slave's body and is to be assumed by all slaves when challenged by a free person, unless of course they are already in the charge of someone else.

I blushed at the shame implicit in the order and she grinned wickedly at my humiliation but I didn't hesitate and moved over to the first of my former friends and assumed it. I now realise that there wasn't a one of these people who had believed my protestations of innocence and this was why they had all accepted Frederica's invitation very willingly.

I was not permitted to look into his eyes but I felt his looking up and down my body and grinning at my nakedness. "Go on, Billy, feel him down," she said encouragingly. "He is no longer your friend but a common criminal slave and a rapist. He is therefore less than an animal and anything that shames or humiliates him is looked on with favour by the government and in particular the Department of Slave Management, so go ahead. Feel him, fondle him, play with his cock and balls and stare into his face as he feels the utter humiliation at being used in such a way by you, his former friend..."

Billy didn't even hesitate then, reached out to finger my muscles and I realised that all this time he had had a hidden longing for my body for the bulge at his loins told the whole story. And after him, I had to move to each one of them, girls included, and submit to the same shameful physical and very intrusive inspection of my body.

But then, when every one of them had had his or her fun at my expense she invited them to arrange their chairs around a plastic sheet one of her garden slaves now brought over for the next entertainment: my violation at the hands of Roger, who you will recall is the giant black muscleman with the huge dong.

Already primed for his task, at Frederica's signal he strode in, stark naked of course but with his huge cock already at full mast and slamming from side to side like a musician's metronome with each step until he reached me and then slapped my face hard from right to left and then back the other way. I had not been privy to his part in the performance the pair of us were now going to provide for her guests but I knew that whatever it was she required him to do to me, it was under the duress of his slavery to her and I certainly held no reproach towards him for it.

He then pretended to discover my tail and exclaimed in shock that I was permitted to wear such an adornment, quickly spinning my body around so that my back and particularly my buttocks and their tail faced her guests. He then simply grabbed it near the point it entered my anus and yanked it out.

"Aaaeeeooowwwaaaggghhheee!" I screamed as my anus was repeatedly ravaged by the ribs of that dildo as it was forcibly removed – and still my friends showed no sympathy for my plight at all.

"And now kneel before me and take my cock right down your throat, slaveboy," he said as if gloatingly but I knew he was only performing this act because as a slave, like every one of us, he well knew he had to obey a direct order.

I moved on my knees to where he was now standing side on to her guests and told me to begin. I gulped. His cock was a veritable monster, all of twenty-five centimetres long and fifteen centimetres in circumference – that's over four centimetres in diameter. I wasn't sure how I was going to get my lips around it let alone take it right down my throat, but I hadn't bargained on Roger's care for me and his ingenuity. He knew that hard and quick would be one hell of a lot better than slow and gentle and so he simply grabbed my head on both sides, harshly ordered me to open my mouth, and then simply slammed his cock right down my throat until my lips were touching his smoothly naked groin while I struggled with all my strength to push him off.

I didn't have the opportunity to look sideways at my former friends but I sensed they were all exulting at my come-down and this rather erotic display of two male slaves performing sexually for their pleasure.

I'm sure the antics of both of us, Roger and me as he held my head close to his groin and I struggled with all my strength and power to push him off. Alas, he was much stronger than me and in any case was in more of a position to keep me there than I was to break away from it but then after another few seconds he slapped my face and push me off as if I was a dirty rag, standing over me and gloating at his sexual mastery of my body.

"Get up white trash and come back to me on your hands and knees like the useless slaveboy you are…"

I knew in my deepest heart that this was all scripted and stage managed but it was very real in another sense and while I knew I had to play my part it was one of the hardest things I have ever had to do. Accordingly, with just a glance at a couple of my former friends with whom I had had very close relationships, and a real disappointment that not one of these young men and women believed my story that it was all a set-up job, I now moved back to the giant black muscleman on my hands and knees as if I was indeed his slave.

Once again he pushed his still rigid cock down and towards my upward looking face and pointed at it. "Take it, boy, or I will force you to and then hold it in your mouth, cutting off your air supply until you are close to death. Choose, slaveboy…"

I knew what I had to do and opened my mouth and moved it forward over that huge flared cock head then reached up and grabbed his hips and swooped down on it until once again my lips were grazing his lower belly.

You may be wondering how I coped with the nausea and gag reflex that kicks in to prevent us humans taking foreign objects down into our lungs? The answer is that I merely forced my mind to take the lesser of two evils, reasoning that I had coped (eventually) with that first attack and therefore this one had to be easier. I did and now he grabbed my head again and began jerking his cock a few centimetres out and then rammed it back in again while my head and body moved with his fuck-fuck motions.

It was extremely shameful and humiliating but by this time I had now put those emotions right out of my mind. In any case, I now realised that these former friends were just that: *former* friends for it was clear they harboured no such emotion towards me anymore.

But then it was time for the final act in this drama. Roger withdrew from my mouth and then directed me to position myself on my hands and knees side on to Frederica's guests while he stood in front of them, legs slightly apart and showing off the beauty of his left bicep muscle flexed while striking his chest with his right fist and then jerking his still erect cock up into the air a few times and grinning suggestively at his audience. All this I could see quite readily from my position kneeling beside him.

By now my arsehole was pulsing in fear at what I knew was now going to be invading it and I wasn't wrong. Roger strode around me a couple of times showing off the magnificence of his tall stature, beautifully wrought musculature and fine skin but then after the final revolution, he dropped down behind me and after splitting into his hand and lubricating his cock, simply drove it forcefully in through my gaping anus and then laid his upper body up my back, his mouth near my right ear and whispering two words: "Courage, Peter."

I was immensely grateful for those two words and I know it assisted me in taking the now violent onslaught of my backside by this incredible young man whom I now counted as my best friend, perhaps even my only friend for those animals sitting over yonder and giggling as they watched me humiliated and shamed to the core by Frederica, were very definitely no longer my friends.

I was about to add the words 'and her minions' to the above sentence but I desisted because William and Mary Havers were her only paid employees, the rest of her staff being slaves and by now I was fairly sure that both the Havers' and probably all of the slaves seemed to have sympathy for my plight. Not that they showed it, of course. If they had, there is no doubt she would have dismissed the former and thoroughly punished the latter with extended doses of the cane or perhaps even her electric bed.

This is another of her tortures that she delighted in as the shocks cause the body of the slave being punished to react in most spectacular ways. I will do so in a moment but just to complete my report of that day with Roger, his ability as a showman in his pretence of raping me had all of his audience enthralled to the core and they were sitting on the edges of their seats watching avidly as that enormous cock of his, driven by the spectacular muscles of his so perfect body, continued to plough in and out of my rectum with an energy that kept their rapt attention from go to whoa.

And when it was finally over, all of my former friends crowded around Frederica, thanking her for a wonderful day and such a spectacular entertainment to cap it off.

Chapter 3

The Electric Bed! The very words instil either a terrible fear or a sexual excitement in almost every human being. The instrument itself varies from a plain wooden bench on which to secure the victim and a TENS unit to deliver the shocks, to a dedicated platform prewired with tiny plugs at strategic locations so that very short wires may be used to connect the electrodes attached to sensitive parts of the body to the power source which may be contained in an elaborate switchboard with many dials and metres all over its surface.

As she had unlimited resources and as she wanted only the best equipment to punish me for my so-called rudeness to her, she investigated the very best such unit on the market and had it installed in readiness for my various punishments.

The bed component of this unit was comprised of a red gum frame supported on legs of the same hard and very heavy wood so that the victim's body was about seventy centimetres above the floor. It was only thirty centimetres wide and two metres long and the tiny plastic sockets were all colour-coded to match the plugs that were stored in a couple of drawers fitted to the underside of the bed.

On the day she scheduled me to suffer its terrible wiles on my body she first explained to me how it was going to give me exquisite agonies for the whole of that day.

"You will only have two electrodes attached to your body, slave. These are they." She now bent over and drew out one of the drawers I could see situated under the top surface of the bed that contained a dozen or more shortish wires each clearly colour-coded. The two she selected were pink and blue and I noted matching sockets formed part of the longitudinal beams along the two sides of the frame.

She gestured for me to lie down on the bench and again she had Roger, my protagonist of a couple of weeks previously, to assist her. By now I had formed a very pleasing rapport with this young man and although I knew he would be obedient to her orders, underneath that façade he would be very sympathetic to my troubles.

Anyway, at her nod he proceeded to secure my wrists and ankles to the usual Velcro-style manacles that could hold the strongest person securely to the four extremities of the table but left the rest of my body quite free. As I later discovered, this was perfectly intentional as she was going to enjoy watching my body and its muscles reacting to the shocks that were shortly going to torment me for the whole of that day.

The wires she had extracted were quite short, just long enough to reach from the socket, located in the frame adjacent to my loins and having pressed the transparent silicon electrode to a point in my left groin right next to my genitals, she then plugged the other end into its colour-coded blue socket on that side. She then made short work of repeating that action on the other side, this time with the pink wire.

Raising my head and looking down my body those two wires were almost invisible. She strolled around me staring down at my supine body hungrily. I was shocked at that expression on her face. Did it mean she still wanted my body sexually? Apart from her fingers tracing little patterns all over my flesh, to that point, she hadn't shown the slightest sign that she was still interested in me but I didn't have a lot of time to ponder the question as she then moved to the console and twiddled a few dials and switches, one of which provided for due attention by the computer to any testicular chip. This she told me gloatingly as she switched it to the positive position.

"Later on, slave, I am going to have you castrated. Your cock and your balls removed by the use of an elastrator that doesn't require a slave vet but will give you exquisite pain for the first twenty-four hours as it causes the blood to pump into your genital organs but cannot escape and so they swell up horribly, eventually dying for the lack of fresh blood.

"But that's in the future. Right now, I want those organs intact as I am going to use them to give you exquisite pain – like this!" And then pressed a button on her console that activated the punishment mode of my little chip.

Of course I reacted, every muscle in my body went into full tension, far harder than I would be able to make them from my own will. It caused my body to immediately arch up off the table and I could feel my muscles trembling and shaking and while I wanted to scream my heart out, my larynx was also paralysed. She let the button go after only a few seconds, commenting sweetly that she mustn't pre-empt the wonderful pain I was going to 'enjoy' during the rest of that day – and yes, she actually used that word 'enjoy' to describe the agonies I was going to experience – or at least assumed I was.

Of course, as I can imagine you will have already guessed, this was going to be my worst day so far in her ownership – and if so, you would be right.

Having set the parameters for the program that was going to last all day, she left the console (it was situated at the foot of the bench) and drew up a chair by my right side to watch and gloat at my naked body suffering the most horrible pains imaginable – and all at the hands of those two tiny electrodes she had pressed onto my groin on either side of my two testicles.

It didn't take very long and the console started to sputter in that tell-tale way such electrical gadgetry often emits and I immediately screamed, although the scream was short-lived as the shocks quickly paralysed my voice-box. But the effects on the rest of the muscles of my body must have been particularly spectacular. Actually, I can attest to that myself for in this part of the slave quarters of her house she had had a large mirror installed over the bed by fastening it to the ceiling. As I stared up at it I could see the middle parts of my body stretch upwards in a shallow arc, the muscles in my arms and shoulders, and my feet and thighs pushing the centre part of my body up into the air as far as it would go and as the machine sputtered away, I could feel the pain of the shocks as if my body was being beaten with heavy iron bars…

The shocks and the concomitant pain seemed to be affecting it all. It certainly wasn't limited to that area of my groin although the pain to my testicles was absolutely horrific. The nearest I can get to describing it was to liken it to them being squeezed to a pulp in the grip of a very strong man's very large hand.

That first shock seemed to go on for ever and as I stared up at my image in the mirror, I could see the sweat beads beginning to form and to eventually coat my whole body with a gleam that made its muscles seem even more prominent. Frederica obviously thought so too for while it was going on, she allowed her fingers to trace over the patterns of my abdominal and thigh muscles, apparently delighting in the sensations in her fingers.

You may be wondering that she did this with total impunity to the shocks? In my later investigations into such machines as this, I learned that the voltages and current levels delivered to those most sensitive parts need only be very small and certainly not permanently damaging to the body so if you are comparing it with say, the electric chair used in times gone by in some states of the USA, there is no comparison at all. They are two totally different concepts.

Having said that however, they were certainly painful and the way they stimulated every muscle in my body to far greater tension than I was able to achieve from the effects of my own brain. As I said, I have no idea how long it lasted. It felt like hours but must have been more than just a few minutes – perhaps five might be a good estimate, and when it was over at last, my body slumped back down onto the wooden bed, coated in a thick layer of my sweat and shaking visibly from the aftermath.

I felt totally drained. Far worse than that day

digging out the compost pit non-stop – and this had only been around the first five minutes!

In order to take my mind off these so morbid thoughts, I tried to think of nice things. Admittedly it wasn't easy. My parents were adequate – and that's about all you can say in their favour. They provided the necessities, at least up until the time I was charged when they virtually disowned me, not even really listening to my pleas of innocence.

My so-called friends had all deserted me and indeed delighted in taking part in that barbecue wherein I was the principal actor (with my friend Roger as the stooge) in a scene of total degradation and most of them had even congratulated her on dealing with her 'rapist' so adequately.

And so I turned to my cadetship at *The Bulletin* and therein lay very much more pleasant thoughts. I had worked hard at my studies and in the tasks set me at the paper and my editor had indicated that he thought I had a great future as a journalist. These were wonderful thoughts and so I let my mind wander over them during the lulls between the times the Electric Bed actually tortured me.

She had set the time of the session to last the whole day, that is up until 6 PM and so the machine's computer spaced out the actual torture sessions appropriately. She apparently knew when they were scheduled and made sure she came down to what she had dubbed The Electric Bed room to watch as I endured the next one. But she often stayed on after it was over and idly toyed with my body and particularly my cock and balls, or she came early and did the same but then laughing gleefully as the shocks cut in and caused my body to react as I described above.

The nature of those shocks seemed to vary. I can't be sure about this as when they actually arrived, the net result to my body was always the same – it would arch up in that straining curve and every muscle under full tension and shaking or trembling violently from the effects of the electricity coursing through my body.

Don't ask me how this could be when the two electrodes were so close together ranged either side of my groin but it certainly happened as I have described.

My whole body was now sweat-streaked and I'm sure my face must have reflected the near exhaustion even that first shock created in me. But then, as the day progressed and the shocks continued, completely unannounced and at very different intervals, I could feel my mind considering begging her for compassion and a relief from this most terrible of tortures she had thus far inflicted upon me.

But then another part of it reacted angrily and chastised the first part for weakness and lack of courage and that part (or was it those thoughts) receded as if in shame at my weakness. These thoughts and others like them were constantly darting in and around my whole being right through that terrible day but I think that the fact that I was able to control them to a great extent kept me with my sanity intact and my body virtually undamaged from the effects of the shocks.

I certainly don't want to downplay their severity. Without a shadow of doubt and in reflection, I am still of the opinion that that electric torture, simple and all as it was, was by far the worst of the many she inflicted upon me during my time as her slave.

One thing I did notice a few days after that most horrible torture was that the definition of the muscles of my body seemed to have improved out of all sight compared to previously. As I thought about this seriously it suddenly occurred to me that the incredible degree of strain, or perhaps exertion would be a better word, that the shocks created in the motor muscles all over it, a degree of exercise not possible in any other way, might well be the answer to that extraordinary honing and toning on my muscles.

No doubt you are already aware of the two major classes of exercise, isotonic and isometric, the former being light but involving a great deal of movement, whereas the other, the principal one of which is weightlifting, involves greater strain but less movement. A combination of both of these classes of exercise is usually recommended by most physical education teachers and personal trainers.

But what I had conjectured about the almost miraculous transformation of my body into a one that now closely resembled that of Roger, whom I'm sure you will remember I advanced as possibly the most highly athletic human being I had ever seen was still puzzling me. Now, my muscles seem to be as clean and sharp as his and I can also attest to a new feeling of physical pleasure in my own body that had nothing to do with sex – simply an appreciation that all its parts were now in perfect condition and were working sympathetically with one another.

Rubbish! You say? So would I in your place but I didn't notice any similar change in any of my other slave companions on that island. I then began to wonder if her machine could be adapted to provide the stimulus to the muscles but without the concomitant pain and if that was the case, and if the change could be as rapid and remarkable as I was now seeing in my own body, I reasoned that such a machine could result in splendid bodies for whole populations, all over the world.

And as a corollary, the holder of the worldwide patents for it would be a very wealthy person indeed.

But these were all later thoughts. Nevertheless, I used my brain, particularly while the shocks were ripping through the nerves all over my body, to think around the pain and not let it distract these other thoughts and to a large extent, I was successful and I was thus able to continue on with the fiction that I was near death and of course that, added to the involuntary reactions of my muscles to the shocks with all manner of screams and begging and anything else I could devise served to feed that bitch's extraordinary ego and hopefully give me a modicum of relief from her worst excesses.

I shan't go on any more about that day. To do so, would simply be a repeat of what I have written above. Suffice it to say each of the shock sessions was absolutely horrible and something to be avoided at all costs if it is within your power to do so.

Roger actually commented on it to me on one of those rare occasions that we were together and out of her sight and the hearing of others and I replied that I thought that terrible Electric Bed torture might be the reason.

He stared at me for a few seconds and then nodded. "You don't know this, Peter, but I was also at Griffith University, studying electronic engineering. My so-called crime involved tampering with examination results, of which I played no part at all but was framed by a group of co-students who resented both my colour and my athletic prowess.

"Over the months leading up to your case, I overheard her discussing with Mr Havers your impending arrival and although those discussions did not include her plans to charge you with rape and in fact both Mr and Mrs Havers would never have gone along with such an evil plan.

"I have enough dirt on those involved in my false accusations to hopefully reverse my conviction and regain my freedom but in my present situation I have no opportunity to exercise it... But in your case I'm very aware that the time period between you and she entering her bedroom and her screaming out that word was far too brief for you have to achieved an erection and thrust it into her. But for the same reasons as in my case, even if you could convince Mr Havers of your innocence, he is in no position to help you, as I'm sure you understand...?"

"Oh yes, Roger. I do understand. But I believe she has had an element of insanity in her probably from birth and that is why she took such an unreasonable hatred of me simply because I didn't want to be her boyfriend when we were at high school. In watching her now, I believe further that this insanity is developing. Perhaps you have noticed it, too?"

"I have, yes. She is both shorter in temper and more unreasonable in the demands she makes of us slaves. It is nothing like the way she treats you who is now her only source of any real pleasure and it sickens me to observe your suffering and her sadistic delight in it as she tortures you – and then justifies it to herself on the grounds that you were unduly rude to her by not accepting her implied demand that you serve as her boyfriend."

This conversation, brief and all as it was, really bolstered my confidence that if indeed she was deteriorating mentally, perhaps it might lead to a total mental breakdown during which both Roger and I might be able to persuade Mr Havers as to our innocence and report the matter to the DSM as the appropriate authority on slaves.

I might have been clutching at straws but of all the dozen or so people on the island other than he and I, he was the only one I trusted and whom I thought might make an ally if we ever got the opportunity.

But in the meantime, I continued to be 'punished' for my so-called raping of her on about a weekly basis although it certainly wasn't that well-regulated and any time, particularly if she believed, or dreamed up, an offence on my part, at any time at all.

By this time she had a veritable suite of torture rooms growing in number all the time in the slave quarters of the cellars of that vast house. To aid her in these nefarious schemes she had purchased a slave skilled in mechanical engineering. He was considerably older than her normal preference in slaves being in his early 30s and had been a leading toolmaker prior to being convicted of murdering his partner in a fit of jealous rage and sentenced to slavery for life. She didn't care one whit for him but only what he could make for her in designing and fabricating instruments of torture destined for just one person – me.

His name was Barry Williams and she spent quite a lot of time with him discussing both simple and complicated items that he could design on the computer she provided for him and then fabricate in the very well equipped workshop she provided for him in another part of her cellars.

The latest in a growing line of such instruments was nothing more than a large wheel suspended on a stub-axle that was firmly affixed to the back wall of this room. The wheel itself most looked like one of those wooden affairs with which ancient horse drawn carriages were equipped. They stood about two metres in diameter and had wooden spokes and rim which, if the wheel had been destined for service on a road, would have had a steel outer layer to serve as its 'tyre'.

Williams made it so that the wheel could revolve and in fact installed a hidden electric motor as part of the central hub which allowed the wheel to be rotated either very slowly or quite fast, this latter facility tending to bring on nausea in the victim quite quickly.

When it was finished, I was scheduled to be its first victim – not that that is unusual as 99% of the articles Barry Williams invented and created were for me, both Frederica and Mr and Mrs Havers having found that a salutary dose of the cane to the naked buttocks of a recalcitrant slave was quite enough to keep the whole herd under control.

It was actually eight days since I had last been 'punished' for that spurious charge and in the meantime I had continued with my normal pony slave duty backed up with exercises in her gymnasium that her so indulgent parents had provided for her. She was one female who didn't believe that girls should be excluded from the all male gymnastic exercises on such implements as the horizontal or parallel bars or the vaulting horse and she worked out pretty nearly daily keeping her splendid body in perfect condition.

The odd thing was that unlike Roger, she hadn't noticed the rather incredible changes to my physique. Actually, I later discovered she had but not wishing to ever compliment me on anything, simply ignored it. Nevertheless, that incredibly sharp definition that the Electric Bed shocks had created in my body (in my opinion) had been retained simply by continuing on with usual isotonic exercises such as sit ups, pullups and the like to my sessions in the gym, as well of course, as those in which I was harnessed to her nasty little gig with its large plug up my arse and the just slightly too tight cuff around the root of my cock and balls (which you may recall created and maintained a full erection as I trotted and galloped her around the island and along the roads and streets of Southport.

I was led up to the wheel by Roger, whom she now always used as her assistant in torturing me. Whether this was because she had discerned our friendship and desired to punish me further by using him to give me pain and humiliate me or whether it was just coincidence is moot but while it certainly distressed him a little, I was glad of his presence during my tortures for she now always left him to supervise me in enduring them when she wasn't there to watch it herself.

Not that we ever used these occasions to talk to one another. The whole of the slave complex in the cellars of that house were bugged and the entire system was supervised by a very sophisticated computer and its program that would alert both her and Mr and Mrs Havers to the infraction, allowing one or all of them to be on the scene in seconds.

Williams had provided a fold-down step that was affixed immediately below the bottom of the wheel and Roger now bent over and lowered the step part of this out and down then turned me around and bade me step back up and onto it. He joined me on it and now reached up to secure my wrists to Velcro manacles attached to the outer rim at 10 o'clock and 2 o'clock respectively and then stepped off it and knelt down to draw my left leg out so that my ankle could be similarly secured at 4 o'clock and lastly, did the same to the other at 7 o'clock.

He then folded the step up and locked it, handing the key to Frederica and then stepped back out of the way. She stood there staring up at my now spreadeagled body in satisfaction. You may be wondering why such an implement might even be considered when there was already that frame in which I could be secured in this manner in another part of the cellar. The answer to that is that little electric motor inbuilt into its hub and she now fished its controller out of her pocket and pressed the button to start the wheel turning.

At first, I felt no sensation at all but then as the minutes passed, I began to feel just a little nauseous and my head to spin in a very unpleasant way and I knew if this continued for much longer I would probably vomit up my morning ration of Slave Chow.

That didn't become necessary because she now stopped it just at the moment my head was at the lowest point. She now stepped up and began to feel and fondle my body in that inverted position, remarking to no-one in particular how pleasant it was to be able to feel and fondle a criminal rapist in any way she wished – and at that moment, grab my balls and pulled them hard out from my body.

"Aaaeeeooowwwaaaggghhheee!" I screamed and once again, I think every muscle in my body went into severe strictures which pleased her even more and so she kept up the pressure on my testicles while looking at Roger to ensure he was not showing any sympathy for me.

Of course he wasn't. He is a highly intelligent young man and I have to say at this point that of late, I found myself becoming attracted to him – yes in that way! She had so controlled my body and particularly denied me any sexual release while at the same time flaunting the beautifully athletic bodies of her female slaves in front of me and even having them and sometimes males as well engage in sexual activities in front of me, simply to tease my libido to the utmost and yet deny me any release.

Tiring of this eventually, she now ordered him

to take my cock in his mouth and to work it … but not on any account to allow me sexual release. I had now been there almost two months and not once in the time had I been permitted to come to sexual climax.

Since obtaining my freedom I have read extensively on how male slaves may be 'chastised'. In this sense, that word does not mean punished but the process of having chastity forcibly imposed upon one. Many male slaves (and some female) are permanently fitted with chastity devices which keep them permanently horny but totally unable to come to any form of climax except that induced by means other than exciting the penis.

At that point neither of us believed ourselves to be in any way homosexually inclined despite that barbecue when he and I were forced to engage in homosexual anal intercourse and that was most definitely not a pleasurable occasion for either of us.

Nevertheless, he stood in front of me with his naked cock very close to my face and took the head of mine into his mouth while his fingers roved up and down my thighs and buttocks while she stood critically to one side watching excitedly as he took all of my cock right down his throat.

At that time, I made no attempt to reach out with my mouth and do the same to his but then it occurred to her that that would be yet another cross for me to bear and so ordered it. I didn't like it. In fact I probably hated it as my lifetime ethics and sexuality all told me this was wrong. Later. Very much later, we both laughed over that event but I don't want to jump the gun so I will leave that comment there.

Now she took to his buttocks with a cane, swiping it hard and encouraging him to feed his cock harder into my mouth while she then snarled at him to take all of my cock down his throat.

From the foregoing, you will have understood that she was now including him in the same horrible tortures to which she had subjected me ever since purchasing me all those months ago. I really felt for him on these occasions but, wonderful friend that he became, he was able to absorb them by using his fine mind in roughly the same way that I had developed to divert the pain she so delighted in inflicting on me by thinking of nice things and more and more he was the object of those things.

In later researching homosexuality, I came upon the startling theory that every human being has a degree of it in their psyche or make-up and that the extent or even the possibility of it coming to the surface very much depends on heredity as well as conditions around the person and his life experiences.

In my case, for example, if I had never become involved with Frederica Masters, it might never have surfaced at all and the same thing applies to Roger Scott. But as it was, and also perhaps because except for her having her slaves perform for her after her own lonely dinner by herself in that house, they too were debarred from casual sexual events with each other.

I was most often used as the recipient for these little shows, especially when they involved the corporal punishment of the slave concerned. She delighted in caning me viciously, especially by ordering me to extend my body along the caning bench without my ankles and wrists being secured but that with the condition that I had to take each of the strokes delivered at full power to my naked buttocks without moving a muscle or uttering even a whimper, and in default, have another six strokes added to the original number.

This sounds like an impossible situation doesn't it? But I soon learned how to control my emotions and the physical aspects of my body to obviate such an unfair but effective disciplinary regime. And later, Roger was able to take a leaf out of my book and so avoid the worst excesses of her now rapidly developing sadistic practices.

This was a new development in that household however and Roger told me on another of those rare occasions we were able to speak with one another privately, that it was causing unrest in the slave quarters. I asked him if he thought it might develop into a real rebellion but he shook his head. "I doubt it, Peter, but they aren't happy…"

Barry Williams continued to dream up, design and fabricate more devices with which she could impose painful torture that included humiliation on me particularly, but now more and more involving Roger as well.

Her after-dinner entertainments which, as I mentioned above, were a new development in that household, now pretty well exclusively involved him and me but increasingly in humiliating practices rather than exclusively painful or demanding of the use of our muscles.

For example, one which I suspect Barry Williams put her up to, was having me lick his arse after having suffered him depositing an artificially induced load of his very sloppy turds onto my face.

We later learned that Barry had explained to her that certain dietary additives could induce such a result especially when the subject had been forced to consume a large quantity of overcooked boiled rice laced with powerful laxatives which makes for a rapid and copious deposit which may be added to by artificially bottling up the donor with a large, cone-shaped buttplug to go on with. All this brings on acute lower belly pain and she learned to delight in subjecting the pair of us to this as a forerunner to the so horrible finale to the scene.

That she achieved from another of Williams' creations. It was a mock-up of a clear plastic portable toilet but with an aperture provided at the front of it into which the recipient (me of course) had to place his neck which was then sealed in place by a sliding door that dropped down in slots to seal him permanently there until released. His face was now situated a mere ten centimetres from the buttocks of the seated donor above him. The clear nature of the apparatus allowed a perfect view of the donor-slave and below him, the recipient, the pair of them forced into this situation at the beginning of the dinner, the donor's rear end being sealed with the large conical butt-plug but of course his belly and bowels churning from the distress brought on by the masses of overcooked rice and accompanying laxatives.

Remember, slaves were normally fed Slave Chow which is a very healthy if uninteresting foodstuff and to be forced to consume masses of the soggy rice laced with those powerful laxatives was a real horror to their systems.

And so as she slowly consumed her dinner with the pair of us already arranged with me underneath Roger and he moaning and groaning from what they had fed his belly and me lying there awaiting something that while not painful was far, far worse than pain. I'm not sure if you can comprehend just how horrible that hour of waiting really was. The event itself was so disgusting as to be almost unmentionable but I want this to be a true account of everything that happened to me under her diabolical ownership and this episode really takes the cake, I think.

Once she had finished her meal, she thanked Mr Havers and then asked him to proceed with my punishment for she still continued with the fiction that I was being punished for raping her.

He acknowledged her order formally and then moved around to assist Roger up from the clear plastic seat then reached under him to jerk the plug from his anus and then quickly pushed him back down onto the seat, retreating as quickly as he could.

I'm sure I don't need to detail the horror of that mass of near-liquid slimy faeces now jetting down on my face. My wrists had been secured behind my back and my body immobilised. I could go nowhere or do anything at all to obviate Roger's turds raining down upon my face almost as a jet.

Yes I could move my head slightly from side to side but that did little but spread the disgusting filth all over my head. I had to do it in order to breathe, of course but all through it, and I'm not sure how many minutes it took but seemed like hours, she sat there and gloated. I know this because he later told me.

I think that little episode encapsulates very neatly just how much her mind had deteriorated over the now six months of her ownership of me.

Just to finish off that tale of woe, she stormed off after Roger had finally spat out his last little jet, disappointed that it was all over and Mr Havers had a couple of slaves on hand to clean up Roger's backside and to get me up and off that diabolical latrine and down to the slave cleaning room and under an extended shower, cold of course as slaves were not permitted hot water for their ablutions, but very welcome to remove the stench and the very idea of Roger's faeces all over my head.

Mr Havers even allowed us to hug one another after that shower which is a mark of the sympathy he really held for me.

Chapter 4

She now lived in solitary splendour as the chatelaine of that beautiful house. She had no visitors and had now ceased to take me over to the mainland to trot me around the streets and show me off as her naked pony slave.

But she certainly hadn't forgiven me and in fact I think her paranoia was getting worse still.

About once a week she forced me to endure more of those electric shocks with the two small clear plastic pads pressed onto my groin beside my genitals and then enjoy the antics of my still near-perfect musculature as the shocks tore into my body.

In labelling my physique in that way I am not in any way, shape or form boasting about its perfection. As I mentioned before, both Roger and I were now very much of the opinion that those electric shocks had been both the root and cause of that development. No other slave on the island was subjected to it and no other slave achieved that incredible development that I now boasted – although I didn't – boast that is.

I was never permitted to forget that I was the lowest of the low even in the slave hierarchy which was in any case at the bottom of the pile. She continually informed me what a piece of dung I was. Fit for nothing but the worst and lowest forms of labour and for whom the most horrible forms of punishment were very necessary.

Caning my buttocks whilst stretched along that form with no restraints holding my wrists and ankles and required to make no sound whatsoever or to even move my body on pain of a further six strokes, was a favourite of hers and as she had, despite all her other problems, kept her body as fit and strong as ever, the pain of that cane administered by her powerful shoulder and arm muscles was a horrible event.

But even worse was when she made me lie on my back on that same bench and then draw my knees up to my chest and spread them as wide as I could thus exposing my anus and then she made Roger, whom she had now decided meant a lot to me, give me six strokes of the cane to my anus.

The buttocks have for centuries been the target for a cane but I am sure you can imagine how much worse the so sensitive and tender ring of muscle that makes up the anus in us humans is very much more susceptible than the buttocks and just a couple of strokes is enough to have the victim screaming in agony.

But if he pulled even one of those strokes, he was told that I would be suspended upside down, a metal funnel inserted into my anus and boiling water poured in. None of us there on the island from Mr and Mrs Havers down, now doubted her words and I think the only reason that they didn't resign and leave her was because they felt their presence did at least effect some measure of restraint on her actions, no matter how small it might be.

I know that Roger and I, still restricted to those very short and seldom possible little exchanges, wanted them to stay no matter how little they were able to tone down the worst of her excesses with Roger and me.

67

He was the only other source of comfort and support to me in those terrible months. No longer did she use me as her pony but she did delight in forcing me into more and more bizarre tails and I now had another horrible duty to perform for her after each movement of her water or her bowels.

I had to attend on both those functions and then if it was the former, reach in and lick her vagina until she permitted me to stop. Now you might imagine that just a couple of licks would be sufficient to clean away any remaining urine. Not a bit of it. I had to kneel there with my hands on her hips and stare up at her adoringly and continue to lick until she decided she had had enough.

As if that wasn't bad enough, when she did the other job, she never ever wiped herself with toilet paper but seated herself on a new chair Barry Williams had created for her that allowed her to lean back and raise her feet up on to rests he created at either side thus exposing her anus beautifully for my attentions.

And as with the other job, I had to lick and lick and lick her anus and of course push my tongue right inside it and wiggle it around ceaselessly while she told me what a horrible little turd I was, fit only for such duties as this and that it wouldn't be long now before she decided to call the slave vet and have me castrated.

Now you may recall that in informing me of this action very early in the piece, she had indicated she would do it herself using an elastrator which is simply an implement used for a century or more by farmers wishing to castrate newly-born male lambs and calves.

It looks a little like a pair of pliers except that it has four hook-shaped prongs over which a special rather thick and very powerful rubber band is slipped. The mechanism allows the handles to be successively pressed and released, pressed and released, gradually opening the four hooks into a square which may then be slipped over the testicles and scrotum of the animal to be castrated and released and within a week or so they drop off from loss of blood and the job is done.

With male slaves however, enterprising owners sometimes decided that a castrated slave would look even better without his penis as well and so a procedure was developed that involved the insertion of a stainless steel catheter up the urethra right into the urinary tract and held there by a tiny hook at the very end of the catheter which when pushed in past the meatus at the end of the penis will catch on the inner lining of the urethra and prevent its exit.

The elastrator with its already prepared stretched rubber band may now be slipped up the penis and each testicle in turn drawn through the rubber band which is then pushed up right against the flesh of the lower groin and released.

The band then slips off the four hooks and tightens around the root of both organs, that is the penis as well as the scrotum and its contents. It is a simple operation and may be carried out by a slave owner himself if he wishes.

But in my case, Frederica wanted to go one step further. She wanted what remained of my urinary tract to be converted into a realistic female vagina. This, she told me, was the perfect punishment for a rapist and once I had been successfully treated she was going to have me exhibited around the country to demonstrate what ought to happen to every male human convicted of sexual offences.

I stared at her in absolute horror but I didn't beg. By now I knew that would merely bring on an immediate execution of the sentence she had just bestowed upon me and so I merely acknowledged her decision with the usual acquiescence of a slave: "Yes, Mistress. It is no more than I deserve."

Abject nonsense, you think. Think again. I was desperate. I don't know if she had an elastrator in the house but they were readily available from all slave emporia and even agricultural suppliers although of course with her wish to have what remained of my genital organs converted as described above, a slave veterinary surgeon would be required.

These professionals were all qualified medical doctors but with the added specialty of training in matters reserved for slaves. Castration is a perfect example. Her slaves were all very healthy and during the time I spent on the island she had never had to call on his services but that didn't mean she wouldn't and in her present state of advanced madness I thought one bad word from me and she wouldn't hesitate.

But still she managed to put on a façade of normality. Not that it was necessary as the only free people she saw now were Mr and Mrs Havers. And if she did call on the slave vet, he wouldn't turn a hair at being requested to castrate me in the way she described. There were many ladies who purchased muscular young bloods like me as their personal slave and some of them delighted in having him castrated as I described as there was then no chance whatsoever that he might make some attempt at a sexual advance to them.

Inasmuch as some of these ladies liked to have their personal slave attend them when out shopping in the larger department stores and the like, their naked slave with no genital organs at all and perhaps just a tiny bud from which they could urinate was quite a common sight.

He would be attending closely upon her because his chip would be conditional on not being further than two metres from her body, in default of which he would suffer an automatic punishment zap to his testicle – or in this case the remaining nerve that would make him think that his non-existent gonad was being squeezed. Brilliant technology, isn't it?

But to get back to Frederica Masters, her whole life now revolved around punishing me and using Roger to shame and hurt me even more as she now recognised that we were very close and he was therefore the perfect means of hurting me.

And so if she perceived I had failed her in some way she would order him to lie down on that bench and for me to cane him at the full strength of my now extraordinarily strong muscles. And if I refused, she told me she would have him castrated rather than me.

And so this threat now loomed over both of us.

Mr Havers tried his best to temper her extremes and to some extent he and his wife were successful and we were both very grateful for his efforts. Without them she might resort to even more horrors such as dipping us into a vat of boiling oil. That horrible man, Barry Williams was now her favourite companion and they talked endlessly about more and more dreadful punishments and tortures.

The only thing that remained normal in her life was her dedication to gymnastics and she now spent more and more time in her gym exercising on the horizontal and parallel bars, the Roman rings (at which she was particularly skilful at) and this was the one time that she was relatively civil to Roger and me because we were both pretty close to Olympic class gymnasts ourselves and she knew we were useful to her in improving her own form.

We too were grateful for those hours because she didn't want Williams there watching her. I understood that. Her body was close to perfect. In fact I have never before or since seen a female with such a perfect physique.

She was certainly no muscle woman. I think they are rather ugly with the enormous muscles that look so out of place on a lady. Frederica's muscles were perfect and in just the right proportion for her physique.

And when she exercised in the gym, she did so naked, quite happy in those hours to treat Roger and I as equals and completely forget my so-called offence to her. Weird is it not? But it's clear given the circumstances I have just enumerators that she didn't want Barry Williams anywhere near her at those times.

He is a very competent toolmaker and can design and fabricate just about anything she (or he) dreams up but he is not a nice looking person. As a slave himself, he is required to be naked but as she delights in perfect physiques in all of her slaves, he is a total aberration to that ideal. His body is short and misshapen; his face is ugly and he generally assumes a scowl as his normal expression. Only in her presence does he ever smile and when he does it just makes everything worse.

She tolerates him because he is a fund of ideas in ways to punish me when she's not in her physical training mode when she is almost pleasant to Roger and me.

I know you are beginning to have doubts about my sanity. The things I am describing are so bizarre as to be pretty well incredulous but when this account is completed, I am going to have Roger and Havers check it for authenticity before locking it away in my safe for posterity. All right, I know I am letting the cat out of the bag to some extent but then you must have already realised that if I am writing this account it is because we finally got free of her. That is not yet however, and I have a little ways to go before I can reveal the ending which is a great deal happier than the months Roger and I suffered under her macabre regime.

During it all he was my only source of any hope whatsoever. Not that he ever came across as a sympathetic friend might. Such behaviour if witnessed by anybody and reported to her would merit God knows what punishment but I suspect would include radical castration for the pair of us.

No, the support he gave me was of the silent and outwardly unemotional kind. Just a look or a half smile was enough to tell me that he was there for me. I don't think at this point that we thought of ourselves as lovers. We were both still, at least nominally, heterosexual although of course she made us perform homosexual acts with each other quite often.

To what extent those acts changed our attitudes to homosexual love, I don't know. I suspect it might have been growing even without us being forced to fuck one another both orally and anally at her whim. On the other hand I must say that I did come to enjoy those encounters with him particularly as female slaves were totally off-limits to us and in fact, she actually got rid of hers, replacing them with more very nicely-muscled young male slaves who also served her personally from time to time.

A weird household?

You bet your bottom dollar it was!

I think deep down she probably was well aware of it which is why she rarely now had visitors. Only her lawyer, investment advisers and any tradesmen necessary for the household ever gained admission to the island.

You may be wondering that in all of this I haven't mentioned sex with her. I should have for it is crucial to her weird psyche. You may recall that from the very beginning of this account, I have tried to indicate her desire to be dominant in everything she engaged herself in and that was the reason that she became so enraged at my rejection of her as her high school boyfriend once she had chosen me.

I think the very idea of her submitting to a man in her bed was so much an infringement of that dominance that was a major part of her psyche as to be totally abhorrent to her and so when she wanted to have sex and I don't think she cared much whether it was with an attractive woman or a handsome man, she would strap on her fucking harness, as she called it, and then required the female or male to submit to her.

I imagine that in her youth and before her parents died she would have found it difficult to find partners willing to submit to this rather weird trait in a woman and particularly one as attractive as her. But I think it was a very predominant part of her psyche. She simply couldn't bear the idea of not being in charge.

And so once her parents died and she assumed mastery of their household, she was able to use her slaves for her own sexual pleasure without restraint. In the early days, I was often used and required either to lie on her bed and draw my knees up to my chest to have my arsehole fucked by her huge fake cock or on other occasions she bent me over and locked my neck and wrists in a frame she had in her bedroom and then fucked my arse in that way until she was sated.

I know I have been particularly crude in the language I have used in this account thus far. That is perfectly intentional. Using polite language to describe the events that she engendered on that island after the death of her parents would make a mockery of the evil that she perpetrated on everyone in her household and who came into contact with her. I used to be sickened by the way her lawyer and her financial advisors crawled to her simply because she was a billionaire.

In the same way though, I admired both Mr and Mrs Havers for their ability to be respectful but not fawning or otherwise obsequious in their dealings with her. As I've said before, I also admired them for their ability to tone down some of her more bizarre ideas as far as they respected Roger and me. Without them I doubt I would have lasted through to the final end to this nightmare.

For nightmare it most certainly was. Roger and I no longer slept in the slave quarters in the cellars. She now ensconced us in her suite but if you think we were given a bed or even a cot to sleep on, think again! Her mania to dominate was always strongest with the pair of us.

It had started with me but gradually spread to Roger as she understood how important he was to me. The examples I have given of him being made to shit on my face is a perfect example of just how bad things were with her mind.

I have read much of the psychology of people like her and am astonished that the human psyche can become so warped by power and/or money (which are really synonymous anyway).

But it was certainly warped with her.

So far as our sleeping quarters is concerned, she had a cage built by Barry Williams that could be covered by a curtain but was normally open so that any visitors to her suite could see just how bizarre was the way she kept us at night.

The cage was made of iron bars such as one might find in those old American Western movies where they formed cells to hold prisoners. The similarity is very moot. The difference is not. The cage is very shallow, no more than half a metre and is only a single metre wide. The entry is from one side and we are required to walk in, turn and poke our cock and balls through a small ring that is then tightened around them. The narrow door is then closed and locked although that is quite unnecessary since we are locked in place there by that ring around our genital organs.

And there we had to stand and try to sleep as she luxuriates in her huge king-size bed with all manner of soft pillows and warm doonas while we stand and shiver side-by-side and try to get some rest.

Only the ingenuity of Mr Havers in postulating to her that we were now useless as domestic slaves for we were too tired to stay awake for very long, made her see reason and we were permitted to sleep on the floor with a blanket around our naked bodies which was just about luxury personified as compared to what we had been through for the last week.

Things were now becoming more desperate for the other slaves, too. Whereas she had always invented offences for me, now she began to do the same with them and both the butler and his wife were now spending an enormous amount of time trying to placate her so unreasonable demands so as to ease the terrible strain now being felt by all of the slaves on the island.

Now again she took to harnessing me to her gig and driving me at a breakneck pace around the track that encircled the island looking for slaves slacking or talking to one another or whatever and I know Mr Havers and his wife were now spending an enormous amount of time trying to talk her out of punishing the slaves for no reason at all.

That isn't to say that Roger and I didn't suffer the cane and other punishments very regularly. Her favourite was that Electric Bed and while it hurt like hell, I didn't mind in another way because it alone, and I suspect even if I had abandoned all other forms of exercise, what that thing did to my body was absolutely incredible. Again I assure you I am not boasting. To do so would be as far from my nature as is possible to be, but I am sure Roger agrees with me that both of our physiques have to be absolutely perfection personified.

I stress again that neither of us could be described as musclemen. I've already said such men and women are not at all attractive in my opinion. What they do with their bodies is their business but from my point of view, an athletic physique is far more attractive than their huge muscles and his and my bodies were absolutely incredible. I don't think it would be possible to improve either of us at all.

I have already said that Roger had been an electronic engineering student and he had set his mind to trying to co-relate the shocks that machine gave our bodies with the effect on them. As often as we could, we discussed it but knew that we were going to have to consult with students of anatomy and physical education in order to suss out exactly what those shocks were doing to our bodies and whether we could modify them to achieve the same result without the awful pain we had to suffer on a regular basis.

Why? Because we had decided that if we could by some miracle get free of her and that island, we would seriously investigate this phenomenon and if we found the answer, develop a machine that would revolutionise the whole basis of physical education, exercise and physique development, take out patents and set up factories that we could hopefully spread across this country, and eventually, around the world.

A pipedream, you believe? Perhaps it was but it was a major plank in our attempts to keep sane during her appalling torture sessions on our bodies. To this end, I quietly and surreptitiously trained Roger in my method of sidelining the pain and thinking of other things but at the same time putting on an exaggerated charade that was authentic enough to keep her delighted in our agony.

Where did I discover this myself? No doubt you have heard of that old saw, '*Necessity is the mother of invention*'? That is really the only answer I can give. It just hit me very early in my slavery to her that I had to develop some means of making her believe I was in agony and at the same time compartmentalise the pain and hide it away in a sort of insulated box. I know it sounds implausible but it's something that worked and once he had mastered it as well, Roger found it a wonderful means of bearing each agony as she and the despicable Barry Williams dreamed them up for us.

In this manner, our lives continued, the best part of them being our gymnastics sessions when she actually appeared normal and interacted with Roger and me almost as if we were her guests on the island.

The fact that she always exercised naked added to this illusion and then when she decided to add wrestling into the mix, it got even better as her moods and manners now seemed to be moving back towards her old happy self. I say this because although she always wanted to be on top, she was good company and those of us in her group really delighted in her companionship.

You may think that if Roger and I exerted our full strength in wrestling with her, she could never win? That is simply not true. I have already said she was both tall, athletic and very strong and while in most cases females are generally weaker than we males, I think she was exceptional and her lithe and distinctly muscular physique enabled her to grapple with each of us to such an extent that we both had to exert just about all of our physical strength to beat her – and often didn't.

Neither of us simply allowed her to win. She wouldn't have wanted that as she was certainly no cheat in this as in everything else and she wanted to win those bouts on the level. I have to say that on the occasions I fought with her, the feel of her muscular naked flesh against my own certainly inflamed me and she was both amused and pleased at the state of my cock as I twisted around, this way and that and our flesh co-mingled constantly.

But she also delighted in gesturing for Roger and me to wrestle and again we both exerted ourselves to the limit. By now, we were pretty nearly equal in strength and muscular development and were a good match so far as wrestling is concerned.

Of course in this case the winner was required to fuck the arse of the loser and to do that just as violently as we had engaged in the wrestling.

I think the sight of our two bodies grappling and straining and thus showing off our so well-defined muscles was something she came to really